Text © 1992 Maggie Russell
Illustrations © 1992 Anthony Lewis
Published exclusively for
Safeway
6 Millington Road, Hayes, Middx UB3 4AY
by Julia MacRae Books
a division of Random House
20 Vauxhall Bridge Road
London SW1V 2SA

First published 1992

Printed in Hong Kong

ISBN 1-85681-016-X

The Three Bears'
Christmas
Party

MAGGIE RUSSELL & ANTHONY LEWIS

SAFEWAY SUPERBOOKS

It was Christmas time and the three bears who lived in the house on the edge of the wood decided to give a party.

They each wrote invitations to their friends. The Great Huge Bear wrote great huge invitations; the Middle-sized Bear wrote middle-sized invitations and the Little Wee Bear wrote little wee invitations (mostly to rabbits).

Then they cleaned the house from top to bottom and decorated it with holly and mistletoe.

"We need a Christmas Tree," said Great Huge Bear. "Tomorrow I'll go out into the wood and dig one up."

Middle-sized Bear who was longing to have a day on her own in the kitchen to do all the cooking said, "Little Wee Bear can go with you. I'll give you both a packet of sandwiches."

In the morning after Great Huge Bear and Little Wee Bear set off, Middle-sized Bear got her cooking pots and her scales and butter and flour from the cupboard and she made Bath buns and rock buns and soft batch buns and whole wheat buns and some great huge Derby Scones and some little wee doughnuts. And she enjoyed herself very much.

Meanwhile Great Huge Bear and Little Wee Bear had gone deep into the wood and had found the perfect tree. First they sat down and ate their sandwiches and then Great Huge Bear took his spade and began to dig in a circle round the roots of the tree.

All at once the spade hit a large stone; it flew up in the air and Great Huge Bear fell onto his back with his leg bent underneath him.

Little Wee Bear was very alarmed. He tried to
help Great Huge Bear to his feet for his knee was
badly twisted.

It took them a long time to get home. Middle-
sized Bear was looking for them anxiously.

She made Great Huge Bear soak his leg in hot water. Then she bandaged it up and said he must go to bed.

"What about the party?" wailed Small Wee Bear. "And we haven't got a Christmas Tree."

Middle-sized Bear thought of all the buns she had cooked. "We shall still have the party," she said. "Great Huge Bear may be better in the morning."

But in the morning Great Huge Bear had a sore head as well as a bad leg. However, he said grumpily that he would come downstairs and sit by the fire.

The guests came promptly at three o'clock.
There were black bears, brown bears and grizzly
bears, the bears from the post office and the bears
from across the stream.

They all arrived together and they all tried to knock on the door at the same time.

There were no rabbits; they were afraid of getting trodden on.

The party was a great success. Everyone made a fuss of Great Huge Bear, who judged the winners of musical bears, musical statues, pass the honey pot and the treasure hunt.

Then they each pulled a cracker and sat down for tea.

As the last bun disappeared and the bears lay back feeling extremely full, there came the sound of squeaky voices singing, *'Good King Wenceslas looked out . . .'*

Little Wee Bear flung open the door and a gang of rabbits giggled nervously. Beyond them stood a Christmas tree.

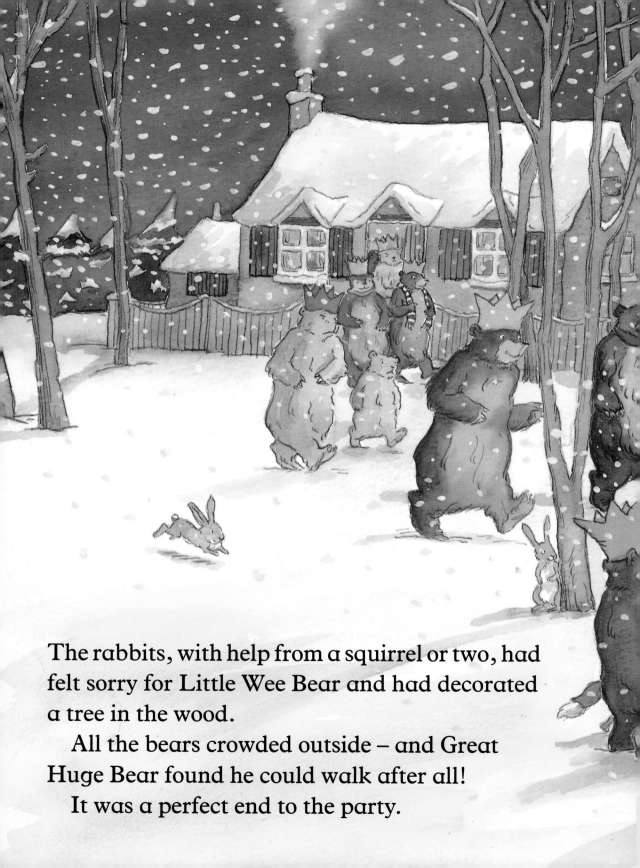

The rabbits, with help from a squirrel or two, had felt sorry for Little Wee Bear and had decorated a tree in the wood.

All the bears crowded outside – and Great Huge Bear found he could walk after all!

It was a perfect end to the party.